THE CLOTHES THEY
STOOD UP IN

Alan Bennett is England's best-loved playwright. He first appeared on the stage in *Beyond the Fringe*. His plays include *Forty Years On*, *Kafka's Dick*, *The Madness of George III*, and an adaptation of *The Wind in the Willows* for the National Theatre. His many television plays include *An Englishman Abroad* and the *Talking Heads* monologues. *Writing Home*, his 1994 prose collection, is still a huge bestseller today. *The Clothes They Stood Up In* originally appeared in the *London Review of Books*. Alan Bennett read the story for Radio 4 for Christmas 1997 and the subsequent BBC tape sold out immediately.

THE CLOTHES THEY
STOOD UP IN

A STORY

BY

ALAN BENNETT

P

PROFILE BOOKS
in association with
LONDON REVIEW OF BOOKS

First published
in book form in Great Britain in 1998 by

PROFILE BOOKS LTD

58A Hatton Garden, London EC1N 8LX

Previously published in 1996 by

LONDON REVIEW OF BOOKS

28 Little Russell Street, London WC1A 2HN

Copyright © Forlake Ltd, 1996, 1998

Second printing 1998

Typeset in Quadraat
Designed by Peter Campbell
Printed and bound in Great Britain by
St Edmundsbury Press Ltd, Bury St Edmunds

Author photo: John Timbers

A CIP catalogue record for this book is available
from the British Library.
ISBN 1 86197 090 0

THE CLOTHES THEY

STOOD UP IN

The Ransomes had been burgled. 'Robbed,' Mrs Ransome said. 'Burgled,' Mr Ransome corrected. Premises were burgled; persons were robbed. Mr Ransome was a solicitor by profession and thought words mattered. Though 'burgled' was the wrong word too. Burglars select; they pick; they remove one item and ignore others. There is a limit to what burglars can take: they seldom take easy chairs, for example, and even more seldom settees. These burglars did. They took everything.

The Ransomes had been to the opera, to *Così fan Tutte* (or *Così* as Mrs Ransome had learned to call it). Mozart played an important part in their marriage. They had no children and but for Mozart would probably have split up years ago. Mr Ransome always took a bath when he came home from work and then he had his supper. After supper he took another bath, this time in Mozart. He wallowed in Mozart; he luxuriated in him; he let the little Viennese soak away all the dirt and disgustingness he had had to sit through in his office all day. On this particular evening he had been to the public baths, Covent Garden, where their seats

7

were immediately behind the Home Secretary. He, too, was taking a bath and washing away the cares of his day, cares, if only in the form of a statistic, that were about to include the Ransomes.

On a normal evening, though, Mr Ransome shared his bath with no one, Mozart coming personalised via his headphones and a stack of complex and finely-balanced stereo equipment Mrs Ransome was never allowed to touch. She blamed the stereo for the burglary as that was what the robbers were probably after in the first place. The theft of stereos is common; the theft of fitted carpets is not.

'Perhaps they wrapped the stereo in the carpet,' said Mrs Ransome.

Mr Ransome shuddered and said her fur coat was more likely, whereupon Mrs Ransome started crying again.

It had not been much of a *Così*. Mrs Ransome could not follow the plot and Mr Ransome, who never tried, found the performance did not compare with the four recordings he possessed of the work. The acting he invariably found distracting. 'None of them knows what to do with their arms,' he said to his wife in the interval. Mrs Ransome thought it probably went further than their arms but did not say so. She was wondering if the casserole she had left in the oven would get too dry at Gas Mark 4. Perhaps 3 would have been better. Dry it may well have been but there was no need to have worried. The thieves took the oven and the casserole with it.

The Ransomes lived in an Edwardian block of flats the colour of ox-blood not far from Regent's Park. It was handy for the City, though Mrs Ransome would have preferred something further out, seeing herself with a trug in a garden, vaguely. But she was not gifted in that direction. An African violet which her cleaning lady had given her at Christmas had finally given up the ghost that very morning and she had been forced to hide it in the wardrobe out of Mrs Clegg's way. More wasted effort. The wardrobe had gone too.

They had no neighbours to speak of, or seldom to. Occasionally they would run into people in the lift and both parties smiled cautiously. Once they had asked some newcomers on their floor round to sherry, but he had turned out to be what he called 'a big band freak' and she had been a dental receptionist with a timeshare in Portugal, so one way and another it had been an awkward evening and they had never repeated the experience. These days the turnover of tenants seemed increasingly rapid and the lift more and more wayward. People were always moving in and out again, some of them Arabs.

'I mean,' said Mrs Ransome, 'it's getting like a hotel.'

'I wish you wouldn't keep saying "I mean",' said Mr Ransome. 'It adds nothing to the sense.'

He got enough of what he called 'this sloppy way of talking' at work; the least he could ask for at home, he felt, was correct English. So Mrs Ransome, who normally had very little to say, now tended to say even less.

When the Ransomes moved into Naseby Mansions the flats had boasted a commissionaire in a plum-coloured uniform that matched the colour of the building. He had died one afternoon in 1982 as he was hailing a taxi for Mrs Brabourne on the second floor, who had forgone it in order to let it take him to hospital. None of his successors had shown the same zeal in office or pride in their uniform and eventually the function of commissionaire had merged with that of caretaker, who was never to be found on the door and seldom to be found any-where, his lair a hot scullery behind the boiler room where he slept much of the day in an arm-chair that had been thrown out by one of the ten-ants.

On the night in question the caretaker was asleep, though unusually for him not in the arm-chair but at the theatre. On the look-out for a classier type of girl he had decided to attend an adult education course where he had opted to study English; given the opportunity, he had told the lec-turer, he would like to become a voracious reader. The lecturer had some exciting, though not very well-formulated ideas about art and the workplace, and learning he was a caretaker had got him tickets for the play of the same name, thinking the resul-tant insights would be a stimulant to group inter-action. It was an evening the caretaker found no more satisfying than the Ransomes did Così and the insights he gleaned limited: 'So far as your actual caretaking was concerned,' he reported to the class, 'it was bollocks.' The lecturer consoled him-self with the hope that, unknown to the caretaker, the evening might have opened doors. In this he was right: the doors in question belonged to the

Ransomes' flat.

The police came round eventually, though there was more to it than picking up the phone. The thieves had done that anyway, all three phones in fact, neatly snipping off the wire flush with the skirting-board so that, with no answer from the flat opposite ('Sharing time in Portugal, probably,' Mr Ransome said, 'or at a big band concert'), he was forced to sally forth in search of a phone box. 'No joke,' as he said to Mrs Ransome now that phone boxes doubled as public conveniences. The first two Mr Ransome tried didn't even do that, urinals solely, the phone long since ripped out. A mobile would have been the answer, of course, but Mr Ransome had resisted this innovation ('Betrays a lack of organisation'), as he resisted most innovations except those in the sphere of stereophonic reproduction.

He wandered on through deserted streets, wondering how people managed. The pubs had closed, the only place open a launderette with, in the window, a pay phone. This struck Mr Ransome as a stroke of luck; never having had cause to use such an establishment he had not realised that washing clothes ran to such a facility; but being new to launderettes meant also that he was not certain if someone who was not actually washing clothes was permitted to take advantage of it. However, the phone was currently being used by the sole occupant of the place, an old lady in two overcoats who had plainly not laundered her clothes in some time, so Mr Ransome took courage.

She was standing with the phone pressed to her dirty ear, not talking, but not really listening either.

'Could you hurry, please,' Mr Ransome said, 'this is an emergency.'

'So is this, dear,' said the woman, 'I'm calling Padstow, only they're not answering.'

'I want to call the police,' said Mr Ransome.

'Been attacked, have you?' said the woman. 'I was attacked last week. It's par for the course these days. He was only a toddler. It's ringing but there's a long corridor. They tend to have a hot drink about this time. They're nuns,' she said explanatorily.

'Nuns?' said Mr Ransome. 'Are you sure they won't have gone to bed?'

'No. They're up and down all night having the services. There's always somebody about.'

She went on listening to the phone ringing in Cornwall.

'Can't it wait?' asked Mr Ransome, seeing his effects halfway up the M1. 'Speed is of the essence.'

'I know,' said the old lady, 'whereas nuns have got all the time in the world. That's the beauty of it except when it comes to answering the phone. I aim to go on retreat there in May.'

'But it's only February,' Mr Ransome said, 'I . . .'

'They get booked up,' explained the old lady. 'There's no talking and three meals a day so do you wonder? They use it as a holiday home for religious of both sexes. You wouldn't think nuns needed holidays. Prayer doesn't take it out of you. Not like bus conducting. Still ringing. They've maybe finished their hot drink and adjourned to the chapel. I suppose I could ring later, only . . .' She looked at the coins waiting in Mr Ransome's hand. 'I've put my money in now.'

Mr Ransome gave her a pound and she took the other 50p besides, saying: 'You don't need money for 999.'

She put the receiver down and her money came back of its own accord, but Mr Ransome was so anxious to get on with his call he scarcely noticed. It was only later, sitting on the floor of what had been their bedroom that he said out loud: 'Do you remember Button A and Button B? They've gone, you know. I never noticed.'

'Everything's gone,' said Mrs Ransome, not catching his drift, 'the air freshener, the soap dish. They can't be human; I mean they've even taken the lavatory brush.'

'Fire, police or ambulance?' said a woman's voice.

'Police,' said Mr Ransome. There was a pause.

'I feel better for that banana,' said a man's voice. 'Yes? Police.' Mr Ransome began to explain but the man cut him short. 'Anyone in danger?' He was chewing.

'No,' said Mr Ransome, 'but...'

'Any threat to the person?'

'No,' said Mr Ransome, 'only...'

'Slight bottleneck at the moment, chief,' said the voice. 'Bear with me while I put you on hold.'

Mr Ransome found himself listening to a Strauss waltz.

'They're probably having a hot drink,' said the old lady, who he could smell was still at his elbow.

'Sorry about that,' the voice said five minutes later. 'We're on manual at the moment. The computer's got hiccups. How may I help you?'

Mr Ransome explained there had been a burglary and gave the address.

'Are you on the phone?'

'Of course,' said Mr Ransome, 'only . . .'

'And the number is?'

'They've taken the phone,' said Mr Ransome.

'Nothing new there,' said the voice. 'Cordless job?'

'No' said Mr Ransome. 'One was in the sitting-room, one was by the bed . . .'

'We don't want to get bogged down in detail,' said the voice. 'Besides the theft of a phone isn't the end of the world. What was the number again?'

It was after one o'clock when Mr Ransome got back and Mrs Ransome, already beginning to pick up the threads, was in what had been their bedroom, sitting with her back to the wall in the place where she would have been in bed had there been a bed to be in. She had done a lot of crying while Mr Ransome was out but had now wiped her eyes, having decided she was going to make the best of things.

'I thought you might be dead,' she said.

'Why dead?'

'Well, it never rains but it pours.'

'I was in one of these launderettes if you want to know. It was terrible. What are you eating?'

'A cough sweet. I found it in my bag.' This was one of the sweets Mr Ransome insisted she take with her whenever they went to the opera ever since she had had a snuffle all the way through Fidelio.

'Is there another?'

'No,' said Mrs Ransome, sucking. 'This is the last.'

Mr Ransome went to the lavatory, only realising when it was too late that the burglary had been so comprehensive as to have taken in both the toilet roll and its holder.

'There's no paper,' called Mrs Ransome.

The only paper in the flat was the programme from Così and passing it round the door Mrs Ransome saw, not without satisfaction, that Mr Ransome was going to have to wipe his bottom on a picture of Mozart.

Both unwieldy and unyielding the glossy brochure (sponsored by Barclay's Bank plc) was uncomfortable to use and unsinkable afterwards, and three flushes notwithstanding, the fierce eye of Sir George Solti still came squinting resentfully round the bend of the pan.

'Better?' said Mrs Ransome.

'No,' said her husband and settled down beside her against the wall. However, finding the skirting-board dug into her back Mrs Ransome changed her position to lie at right angles to her husband so that her head now rested on his thigh, a situation it had not been in for many a long year. While telling himself this was an emergency it was a conjunction Mr Ransome found both uncomfortable and embarrassing, but which seemed to suit his wife as she straightaway went off to sleep, leaving Mr Ransome staring glumly at the wall opposite and its now uncurtained window, from which, he noted wonderingly, the burglars had even stolen the curtain rings.

It was four o'clock before the police arrived, a big middle-aged man in a raincoat, who said he was a detective sergeant, and a sensitive-looking young constable in uniform, who didn't say anything at all.

'You've taken your time,' said Mr Ransome.

'Yes,' said the sergeant. 'We would have been earlier but there was a slight . . . ah, glitch as they say. Rang the wrong doorbell. The fault of mi-lad-do here. Saw the name Hanson and . . .'

'No,' said Mr Ransome. 'Ransome.'

'Yes. We established that . . . eventually. Just moved in, have you?' said the sergeant, surveying the bare boards.

'No,' said Mr Ransome. 'We've been here for thirty years.'

'Fully furnished, was it?'

'Of course,' said Mr Ransome. 'It was a normal home.'

'A settee, easy chairs, a clock,' said Mrs Ransome. 'We had everything.'

'Television?' said the constable, timidly.

'Yes,' said Mrs Ransome.

'Only we didn't watch it much,' said Mr Ransome.

'Video recorder?'

'No,' said Mr Ransome. 'Life's complicated enough.'

'CD player?'

'Yes,' said Mrs Ransome and Mr Ransome together.

'And my wife had a fur coat,' said Mr Ransome. 'My insurance have a list of the valuables.'

'In that case,' said the sergeant, 'you are laughing. I'll just have a little wander round if you don't mind, while Constable Partridge takes down the details. People opposite see the intruder?'

'Away in Portugal,' said Mr Ransome.

'Caretaker?'

'Probably in Portugal too,' said Mr Ransome, 'for all we see of him.'

'Is it Ransom as in king's?' said the constable. 'Or Ransome as in Arthur?'

'Partridge is one of our graduate entrants,' said the sergeant, examining the front door.

'Lock not forced, I see. He's just climbing the ladder. There wouldn't be such a thing as a cup of tea, would there?'

'No,' said Mr Ransome shortly, 'because there wouldn't be such a thing as a teapot. Not to mention a teabag to put in it.'

'I take it you'll want counselling,' said the constable.

'What?'

'Someone comes along and holds your hand,' said the sergeant, looking at the window. 'Partridge thinks it's important.'

'We're all human,' said the constable.

'I'm a solicitor,' said Mr Ransome.

'Well,' said the sergeant, 'Perhaps your missus

20

could give it a try. We like to keep Partridge happy.'

Mrs Ransome smiled helpfully.

'I'll put yes,' said the constable.

'They didn't leave anything behind, did they?' asked the sergeant, sniffing and reaching up to run his hand along the picture-rail.

'No,' said Mr Ransome testily. 'Not a thing. As you can see.'

'I didn't mean something of yours,' said the sergeant, 'I meant something of theirs.' He sniffed again, inquiringly. 'A calling card.'

'A calling card?' said Mrs Ransome.

'Excrement,' said the sergeant. 'Burglary is a nervous business. They often feel the need to open their bowels when doing a job.'

'Which is another way of saying it, sergeant,' said the constable.

'Another way of saying what, Partridge?'

'Doing a job is another way of saying opening the bowels. In France,' said the constable, 'it's known as posting a sentry.'

'Oh, teach you that at Leatherhead, did they?' said the sergeant. 'Partridge is a graduate of the police college.'

'It's like a university,' explained the constable,

'only they don't have scarves.'

'Anyway,' said the sergeant, 'have a scout round. For the excrement, I mean. They can be very creative about it. Burglary in Pangbourne I attended once where they done it halfway up the wall in an 18th-century light fitting. Any other sphere and they'd have got the Duke of Edinburgh's Award.'

'You've perhaps not noticed,' Mr Ransome said grimly, 'but we don't have any light fittings.'

'Another one in Guildford did it in a bowl of this pot-pourri.'

'That would be irony,' said the constable.

'Oh would it?' said the sergeant. 'And there was me thinking it was just some foul-arsed, light-fingered little smackhead afflicted with incontinence. Still, while we're talking about bodily functions, before we take our leave I'll just pay a visit myself.'

Too late Mr Ransome realised he should have warned him and took refuge in the kitchen.

The sergeant came out shaking his head.

'Well at least our friends had the decency to use the toilet but they've left it in a disgusting state. I never thought I'd have to do a Jimmy Riddle over Dame Kiri Te Kanawa. Her recording of *West Side Story* is one of the gems of my record collection.'

'To be fair,' said Mrs Ransome, 'that was my husband.'

'Dear me,' said the sergeant.

'What was?' said Mr Ransome, coming back into the room.

'Nothing,' said his wife.

'Do you think you'll catch them?' said Mr Ransome as he stood at the door with the two policemen.

The sergeant laughed.

'Well, miracles do happen, even in the world of law enforcement. Nobody got a grudge against you, have they?'

'I'm a solicitor,' said Mr Ransome. 'It's possible.'

'And it's not somebody's idea of a joke?'

'A *joke*?' said Mr Ransome.

'Just a thought,' said the sergeant. 'But if it's your genuine burglar, I'll say this: he always comes back.'

The constable nodded in sage confirmation; even Leatherhead was agreed on this. 'Come back?' said Mr Ransome bitterly, looking at the empty flat.

'*Come back*? What the fuck for?'

Mr Ransome seldom swore and Mrs Ransome

who had stayed in the other room, pretended she hadn't heard. The door closed.

'Useless,' said Mr Ransome, coming back. 'Utterly useless. It makes you want to swear.'

'Well,' said Mrs Ransome a few hours later, 'we shall just have to camp out. After all,' she said not unhappily, 'it could be fun.'

'Fun?' said Mr Ransome. 'Fun?'

He was unshaven, unwashed, his bottom was sore and his breakfast had been a drink of water from the tap. Still, no amount of pleading on Mrs Ransome's part could stop him going heroically off to work, with his wife instinctively knowing even in these unprecedented circumstances that her role was to make much of his selfless dedication.

Even so, when he'd gone and with the flat so empty, Mrs Ransome missed him a little, wandering from room to echoing room not sure where she should start. Deciding to make a list she forgot for the moment she had nothing to make a list with and nothing to make a list on. This meant a visit to the newsagents for pad and pencil where, though she'd never noticed it before, she found there was a café next door. It seemed to be doing hot break-

24

fasts, and, though in her opera clothes she felt a bit out of place among the taxi-drivers and bicycle couriers who comprised most of the clientèle, nobody took much notice of her, the waitress even calling her 'duck' and offering her a copy of the *Mirror* to read while she waited for her bacon, egg, baked beans and fried bread. It wasn't a paper she would normally read, but bacon, egg, baked beans and fried bread wasn't a breakfast she would normally eat either, and she got so interested in the paper's tales of royalty and its misdemeanours that she propped it up against the sauce bottle so that she could read and eat, completely forgetting that one of the reasons she had come into the café was to make herself a list.

Wanting a list, her shopping was pretty haphazard. She went off to Boots first and bought some toilet rolls and some paper plates and cups, but she forgot soap. And when she remembered soap and went back for it, she forgot teabags, and when she remembered teabags, she forgot paper towels, until what with trailing halfway to the flats then having to go back again, she began to feel worn out.

It was on the third of these increasingly flustered trips (now having forgotten plastic cutlery) that Mrs Ransome ventured into Mr Anwar's. She passed the shop many times as it was midway between the flats and St John's Wood High Street; indeed she remembered it opening and the little draper's and babies' knitwear shop which it had replaced and where she had been a loyal customer. That had been kept by a Miss Dorsey, from whom over the years she had bought the occasional tray cloth or hank of Sylko but, on a much more regular basis, plain brown paper packets of what in those days were called 'towels'. The closing-down of the shop in the late Sixties had left Mrs Ransome anxious and unprotected and it came as a genuine surprise on venturing into Timothy White's to find that technology in this intimate department had lately made great strides which were unreflected in Miss Dorsey's ancient stock, of which Mrs Ransome, as the last of a dwindling clientèle, had been almost the sole consumer. She was old-fashioned, she knew that, but snobbery had come into it too, Mrs Ransome feeling it vaguely classier to have her requirements passed wordlessly across the counter with Miss Dorsey's patient, suffering smile ('Our cross,' it said) rather than taken from some promiscuous shelf in Timothy White's. Though it was not long before Timothy White's went the same way as Miss Dorsey, swallowed whole by Boots. Though Boots too, she felt, was a cut above the nearest chemist, Superdrug, which didn't look classy at all.

The closing-down of Miss Dorsey's (she was found laid across the counter one afternoon having had a stroke) left the premises briefly empty until, passing one morning on the way to the High Street, Mrs Ransome saw that the shop had been taken over by an Asian grocer and that the pavement in front of the window where nothing had previously stood except the occasional customer's pram was now occupied by boxes of unfamiliar vegetables ... yams, pawpaws, mangoes and the like, together with many sacks, sacks, Mrs Ransome felt, that dogs could all too easily cock their leg against.

So it was partly out of loyalty to Mrs Dorsey and partly because it wasn't really her kind of thing that Mrs Ransome had not ventured into the shop until this morning when, to save her trailing back for the umpteenth time to the High Street, she thought she might go in and ask if they had such a thing as boot polish (there were more pressing requirements, as she would have been the first to admit, only Mr Ransome was very particular about his shoes). Though over twenty years had passed, the shop was still recognisably what it had been in Miss Dorsey's day because, other than having introduced a freezer and cold cupboards, Mr Anwar had simply adapted the existing fixtures to his changed requirements. Drawers that had previously been devoted to the genteel accoutrements of a leisured life – knitting patterns, crochet hooks, rufflette – now housed nans and pitta bread; spices replaced bonnets and bootees and the shelves and deep drawers that once were home to hosiery and foundation garments were now filled with rice and chickpeas.

Mrs Ransome thought it unlikely they had polish in stock (did they wear normal shoes?), but she was weary enough to give it a try though, since oxblood was what she wanted (or Mr Ransome required), she thought vaguely it might be a shade to which they had religious objections. But plump and cheerful Mr Anwar brought out several tins for her kind consideration and while she was paying she spotted a nail-brush they would be needing; then the tomatoes looked nice and there was a lemon, and while she was at it the shop seemed to sell hardware so she invested in a colander. As she wandered round the shop the normally tongue-tied Mrs Ransome found herself explaining to this plump and amiable grocer the circumstances which had led her to the purchase of such an odd assortment of things. And he smiled and shook his head in sympathy while at the same time suggesting other items she would doubtless be needing to replace and which he would happily supply. 'They cleaned you out of house and home, the scally-wags. You will not know whether you are coming or going. You will need washing-up liquid and one of these blocks to make the toilet a more savoury place.'

So she ended up buying a dozen or so items, too many for her to carry, but this didn't matter either as Mr Anwar fetched his little boy from the flat up-stairs ('I hope I'm not dragging him away from the Koran,' she thought) and he followed Mrs Ran-some home in his little white cap, carrying her shopping in a cardboard box.

'Seconds probably,' said Mr Ransome later. 'That's how they make a profit.'

Mrs Ransome didn't quite see how there could be seconds in shoe polish but didn't say so.

'Hopefully,' she said 'they'll deliver.'

'You mean,' said Mr Ransome (and it was old ground), 'you hope they'll deliver. "Hopefully they'll deliver" means that deliveries are touch and go' (though that was probably true too).

'Anyway,' said Mrs Ransome defiantly, 'he stays open till ten at night.'

'He can afford to,' said Mr Ransome. 'He probably pays no wages. I'd stick to Marks and Spencer.'

Which she did, generally speaking. Though once she popped in and bought a mango for her lunch and another time a pawpaw; small adventures, it's true, but departures nevertheless, timorous voyages of discovery which she knew her husband well enough to keep to herself.

The Ransomes had few friends; they seldom entertained, Mr Ransome saying that he saw quite enough of people at work. On the rare occasions when Mrs Ransome ran into someone she knew and ventured to recount their dreadful experience she was surprised to find that everyone, it seemed, had their own burglar story. None, she felt, were so stark or so shocking as to measure up to theirs, which ought in fairness to have trumped outright these other less flamboyant break-ins, but comparison scarcely seemed to enter into it: the friends only endured her story as an unavoidable prelude to telling her their own. She asked Mr Ransome if he had noticed this.

'Yes,' he said shortly. 'Anybody would think it happened every day.'

Which, of course, it did but not, he was certain, as definitively, as out and outedly, as altogether epically as this.

'Everything,' Mr Ransome told Gail, his longtime secretary, 'every single thing.'

Gail was a tall, doleful-looking woman, which normally suited Mr Ransome very well as he could not abide much of what he called 'silliness' – i.e. femininity. Had Gail been a bit sillier, though, she might have been more sympathetic, but like everyone else she weighed in with a burglar story of her own, saying she was surprised it hadn't happened before as most people she knew had been burgled at least once and her brother-in-law, who was a chiropodist in Ilford, twice, one of which had been a ram-raid while they were watching television.

'What you have to watch out for is the trauma; it takes people in different ways. Hair loss is often a consequence of burglary apparently and my sister came out in terrible eczema. Mind you,' Gail went on, 'it's always men.'

'Always men what?' said Mr Ransome.

'Who burgle.'

'Well, women shoplift,' said Mr Ransome defensively.

'Not to that extent,' said Gail. 'They don't clean out the store.'

Not sure how he had ended up on the wrong side of the argument, Mr Ransome felt both irritated and dissatisfied, so he tried Mr Pardoe from the firm next door but with no more success. 'Cleaned you out completely? Well, be grateful you weren't in. My dentist and his wife were tied up for seven hours and counted themselves lucky not to be raped. Balaclavas, walkie-talkies. It's an industry nowadays. I'd castrate them.'

That night Mr Ransome took out a dictionary from his briefcase, both dictionary and briefcase newly acquired. The dictionary was Mr Ransome's favourite book.

'What are you doing?' asked Mrs Ransome.

'Looking up "lock, stock and barrel". I suppose it means the same as "the whole shoot".'

32

Over the next week or so Mrs Ransome assembled the rudiments – two camp beds plus bedding and towels, a card table and two folding chairs. She bought a couple of what she called bean-bags, though the shop called them something else; they were quite popular apparently, even among people who had not been burgled who used them to sit on the floor by choice. There was even (this was Mr Ransome's contribution) a portable CD player and a recording of *The Magic Flute*.

Mrs Ransome had always enjoyed shopping so this obligatory re-equipment with the essentials of life was not without its pleasures, though the need was so pressing that choice scarcely entered into it. Hitherto anything electrical had always to be purchased by, or under the supervision of, Mr Ransome, a sanction that applied even with an appliance like the vacuum cleaner, which he never wielded, or the dishwasher, which he seldom stacked. However, in the special circumstances obtaining after the burglary, Mrs Ransome found herself licensed to buy whatever was deemed necessary, electrical or otherwise; not only did she get an electric kettle, she also went in for a microwave oven, an innovation Mr Ransome had long resisted and did not see the point of.

That many of these items (the bean-bags for instance) were likely to be discarded once the insurance paid out and they acquired something more permanent, did not diminish Mrs Ransome's quiet zest in shopping for them. Besides, the second stage was likely to be somewhat delayed as the insurance policy had been stolen too, together with all their other documents, so compensation, while not in doubt, might be slow in coming. In the meantime they lived a stripped-down sort of life which seemed to Mrs Ransome, at least, not unpleasant.

'Hand to mouth,' said Mr Ransome.

'Living out of a suitcase,' said Croucher, his insurance broker.

'No,' said Mr Ransome. 'We don't have a suitcase.'

'You don't think,' asked Croucher, 'it might be some sort of joke?'

'People keep saying that,' said Mr Ransome. 'Jokes must have changed since my day. I thought they were meant to be funny.'

'What sort of CD equipment was it?' said Croucher.

'Oh, state of the art,' said Mr Ransome. 'The latest and the best. I've got the receipts somewhere . . . oh no, of course. I was forgetting.'

Though this was a genuine slip it was perhaps fortunate that the receipts had been stolen along with the equipment which they were for, because Mr Ransome was telling a little lie. His sound equipment was not quite state of the art, as what equipment is? Sound reproduction is not static; perfection is on-going and scarcely a week passes without some technical advance. As an avid reader of hi-fi magazines, Mr Ransome often saw advertised refinements he would dearly have liked to make part of his listening experience. The burglary, devastating though it had been, was his opportunity. So it was at the moment when he woke up to the potential advantages of his loss that this most unresilient of men began, if grudgingly, to bounce back.

Mrs Ransome, too, could see the cheerful side of things, but then she always did. When they had got married they had kitted themselves out with all the necessities of a well-run household; they had a dinner service, a tea service plus table linen to match; they had dessert dishes and trifle glasses and cakestands galore. There were mats for the dressing-table, coasters for the coffee table, runners for the dining table; guest towels with matching flannels for the basin, lavatory mats with matching ones for the bath. They had cake slices and fish slices and other slices besides, delicate trowels in silver and bone the precise function of which Mrs Ransome had never been able to fathom. Above all there was a massive many-tiered canteen of cutlery, stocked with sufficient knives, forks and spoons for a dinner party for 12. Mr and Mrs Ransome did not have dinner parties for 12. They did not have dinner parties. They seldom used the guest towels because they never had guests. They had transported this paraphernalia with them across 32 years of marriage to no purpose at all that Mrs Ransome could see, and now at a stroke they were rid of the lot. Without quite knowing why, and while she was washing up their two cups in the sink, Mrs Ransome suddenly burst out singing.

'It's probably best,' said Croucher, 'to proceed on the assumption that it's gone and isn't going to come back. Maybe someone fancied a well-appointed middle-class home and just took a short cut.'

He stood at the door.

'I'll get a cheque to you as soon as I can. Then you can start rebuilding your lives. Your good lady seems to be taking it well.'

'Yes,' said Mr Ransome, 'only she keeps it under.'

'No outstanding jewellery or anything of that sort?'

'No. She's never really gone in for that sort of thing,' said Mr Ransome. 'Luckily she was wearing her pearls to the opera.'

'She had a necklace on tonight,' said Croucher. 'Rather striking I thought.'

'Did she?' Mr Ransome hadn't noticed.

When they were at the card table having their supper Mr Ransome said: 'Have I seen that necklace before?'

'No. Do you like it? I bought it at the grocer's.'

'The *grocer's*?'

'The Indian shop. It was only 75p. I can't wear my pearls all the time.'

'It looks as if it came out of a cracker.'

'I think it suits me. I bought two. The other one's green.'

'What am I eating?' said Mr Ransome. 'Swede?'

'A sweet potato. Do you like it?'

'Where did you get it?'

'Marks and Spencer.'

'It's very nice.'

A couple of weeks after the burglary (everything now dated from that) Mrs Ransome was sitting on her bean-bag in front of the electric fire, her legs stuck out in front of her, contemplating her now rather scuffed court shoes, and wondering what she ought to do next. It was the same with a death, she thought: so much to do to begin with, then afterwards nothing.

Nevertheless (and further to her thoughts at the sink) Mrs Ransome had begun to see that to be so abruptly parted from all her worldly goods might bring with it benefits she would have hesitated to call spiritual but which might, more briskly, be put under the heading of 'improving the character'. To have the carpet almost literally pulled from under her should, she felt, induce salutary thoughts about the way she had lived her life. War would once have rescued her, of course, some turn of events that gave her no choice, and while what had happened was not a catastrophe on that scale she knew it was up to her to make of it what she could.

She would go to museums, she thought, art galleries, learn about the history of London; there were classes in all sorts nowadays – classes which she could perfectly well have attended before they were deprived of everything they had in the world, except that it was everything they had in the world, she felt, that had been holding her back. Now she could start. So, plumped down on the bean-bag on the bare boards of her sometime lounge, Mrs Ransome found that she was not unhappy, telling herself that this was more real and that (though one needed to be comfortable) an uncushioned life was the way they ought to live..

It was at this point the doorbell rang.

'My name is Briscoe,' the voice said over the intercom. 'Your counsellor?'

'We're Conservatives,' said Mrs Ransome.

'No,' said the voice. 'The police? Your trauma? The burglary?'

Knowing the counsellor had come via the police Mrs Ransome had expected someone a bit, well, crisper. There was nothing crisp about Ms Briscoe, except possibly her name and she got rid of that on the doorstep.

'No, no. Call me Dusty. Everybody does.'

'Were you christened Dusty?' asked Mrs Ransome, bringing her in. 'Or is that just what you're called?'

'Oh no. My proper name is Brenda but I don't want to put people off.'

Mrs Ransome wasn't quite sure how, though it was true she didn't look like a Brenda: whether she looked like a Dusty she wasn't sure as she'd never met one before.

She was a biggish girl who, perhaps wisely, had opted for a smock rather than a frock and with it a cardigan so long and ample it was almost a dress in itself, one pocket stuffed with her diary and notebook, the other sagging under the weight of a mobile phone. Considering she worked for the authorities Mrs Ransome thought Dusty looked pretty slapdash.

'Now you are Mrs Ransome? Rosemary Ransome?'

'Yes.'

'And that's what people call you, is it? Rosemary?'

'Well, yes' (insofar as they call me anything, thought Mrs Ransome).

'Just wondered if it was Rose or Rosie?'

'Oh no.'

'Hubby calls you Rosemary, does he?'

'Well, yes,' said Mrs Ransome, 'I suppose he does,' and went to put the kettle on, thus enabling Dusty to make her first note: 'Query: Is burglary the real problem here?'

When Dusty had started out counselling, victims were referred to as 'cases'. That had long since gone; they were now clients or even customers, terms Dusty to begin with found unsympathetic and had resisted. Nowadays she never gave either designation a second thought – what her clients were called seemed as immaterial as the disasters that befell them. Victims singled themselves out; be it burglary, mugging or road accidents, these mishaps were simply the means by which inadequate people came to her notice. And everybody given the chance had the potential to be inadequate. Experience, she felt, had turned her into a professional.

They took their tea into the sitting-room and each sank onto a bean-bag, a manoeuvre Mrs Ransome was now quite good at, though with Dusty it was more like a tumble. 'Are these new?' said Dusty, wiping some tea from her smock. 'I was

41

with another client yesterday, the sister of someone who's in a coma, and she had something similar. Now Rosemary, I want us to try and talk this through together.'

Mrs Ransome wasn't sure whether this was the same as 'talking it over'. One seemed a more rigorous, less meandering version of the other, the difference in their choice of prepositions not boding well for fruitful discourse. 'More structured,' Dusty would have said, had Mrs Ransome ventured to raise the point, but she didn't.

Mrs Ransome now described the circumstances of the burglary and the extent of their loss, though this made less of an impression on Dusty than it might have done as the diminished state in which the Ransomes were now living – the bean-bags, the card table etc – seemed not so much a deprivation to Dusty as it did a style.

Though this was more tidy it was the minimalist look she had opted for in her own flat.

'How near is this to what it was before?' said Dusty.

'Oh we had a lot more than this,' said Mrs Ransome. 'We had everything. It was a normal home.'

'I know you must be hurting,' said Dusty.

'Hurting what?' asked Mrs Ransome.

'You. You are hurting.'

Mrs Ransome considered this, her stoicism simply a question of grammar, 'Oh. You mean I'm hurt? Well, yes and no. I'm getting used to it, I suppose.'

'Don't get used to it too soon,' said Dusty. 'Give yourself time to grieve. You did weep at the time, I hope?'

'To begin with,' said Mrs Ransome. 'But I soon got over it.'

'Did Maurice?'

'Maurice?'

'Mr Ransome.'

'Oh . . . no. No. I don't think he did. Well,' and it was as if she were sharing a secret, 'he's a man, you see.'

'No, Rosemary. He's a person. It's a pity that he didn't let himself go at the time. The experts are all more or less agreed that if you don't grieve, keep it all bottled up, you're quite likely at some time in the future to go down with cancer.'

'Oh dear,' said Mrs Ransome.

'Of course,' said Dusty. 'Men do find grieving harder than women. Would it help if I had a word?'

'With Mr Ransome? No, no,' said Mrs Ransome hastily. 'I don't think so. He's very . . . shy.'

'Still,' said Dusty, 'I think I can help you . . . or we can help each other.' She leaned over to take Mrs Ransome's hand but found she couldn't reach it so stroked the bean-bag instead.

'They say you feel violated,' said Mrs Ransome.

'Yes. Let it come, Rosemary. Let it come.'

'Only I don't particularly. Just mystified.'

'Client in denial,' Dusty wrote as Mrs Ransome took away the teacups. Then she added a question-mark.

As she was going Dusty suggested that Mrs Ransome might try to see the whole experience as a learning curve and that one way the curve might go (it could go several ways apparently) was to view the loss of their possessions as a kind of liberation – 'the lilies of the field syndrome', as Dusty called it. 'Lay not up for yourself treasures on earth-type-thing.' This notion having already occurred to Mrs Ransome she nevertheless didn't immediately take the point because Dusty referred to their belongings as 'their gear', a word, which, if it meant anything to Mrs Ransome, denoted the contents of her handbag, lipstick, compact etc, none of which she

44

had in fact lost. Though thinking about it afterwards she acknowledged that to lump everything,
carpets, curtains, furniture and fittings all under
the term 'gear' did make it easier to handle. Still it
wasn't a word she contemplated risking on her
husband.

Truth to tell (and though she didn't say so to
Mrs Ransome) it was advice Dusty only proffered
half-heartedly anyway. The more she saw of the
lilies of the field syndrome the less faith she had in
it. She'd had one or two clients who'd told her that
a hurtful burglary had given them a clue how to
live, that from now on they would set less store by
material possessions, travel light etc. Six months
later she'd gone back on a follow-up visit to find
them more encumbered than ever. Lots of people
could give up things, Dusty had decided; what they
couldn't do without was shopping for them.

When Mrs Ransome said to Dusty that she
didn't particularly miss her belongings she had
been telling the truth. What she did miss – and this
was harder to put into words – was not so much the
things themselves as her particular paths through
them. There was the green bobble hat she had had,
for instance, which she never actually wore but

would always put on the hall table to remind her that she had switched the immersion heater on in the bathroom. She didn't have the bobble hat now and she didn't have the table to put it on (and that she still had the immersion heater must be regarded as a providence). But with no bobble hat she'd twice left the immersion on all night and once Mr Ransome had scalded his hand.

He too had had rituals to forego. He had lost the little curved scissors, for instance, with which he used to cut the hair in his ears – and that was only the beginning of it. While not especially vain he had a little moustache which, if left to itself, had a distasteful tendency to go ginger, a tinge which Mr Ransome kept in check with the occasional touch of hair dye. This came out of an ancient bottle Mrs Ransome had tried on her roots years ago and then instantly discarded, but which was still kept at the back of the bathroom cupboard. Locking the bathroom door before applying it to the affected part, Mr Ransome had never admitted to what he was doing, with Mrs Ransome in her turn never admitting that she knew about it anyway. Only now the bathroom cupboard was gone and the bottle with it, so in due course Mr Ransome's moustache began to take on the tell-tale orange tinge he found so detestable. Asking her to buy another bottle was one answer but this would be to come clean on the years of clandestine cosmetics. Buying a bottle himself was another. But where? His barber was Polish and his English just about ran to short back and sides. An understanding chemist perhaps, but all the chemists of Mr Ransome's acquaintance were anything but understanding, staffed usually by bored little sluts of 18 unlikely to sympathise with a middle-aged solicitor and his creeping ginger.

Unhappily tracing its progress in Mrs Ransome's powder compact, kept in the bathroom now as the only mirror in the flat, Mr Ransome cursed the burglars who had brought such humiliation upon him and lying on her camp bed Mrs Ransome reflected that not the least of what they had lost in the burglary were their little marital deceptions.

Mr Ransome had been told that while the insurance company would not pay for the temporary rental of a CD player (not regarded as an essential) it would sanction the hire of a TV. So one morning Mrs Ransome went out and chose the most discreet model she could find and it was delivered and fitted that same afternoon. She had never watched daytime television before, feeling she ought to have better things to do. However, when he had gone she found the engineer had left the set switched to some sort of chat show in which an overweight American couple were being questioned by a black lady in a trouser suit about how, as the black lady put it, 'they related to one another sexually.'

The man, slumped in his seat with his legs wide apart, was describing in as much detail as the woman in the trouser suit would allow what he, as he put it, 'asked of his marriage', while the woman, arms folded, knees together but too plump to be prim, was explaining how 'without being judgmental, he had never taken the deodorant on board'.

'Get a load of that body language,' said the lady in the trouser suit, and the audience, mystifyingly to Mrs Ransome who did not know what body language was, erupted in jeers and laughter.

'The things people do for money,' thought Mrs Ransome, and switched it off.

The next afternoon, waking from a doze on her bean-bag, she switched on again and found herself watching a similar programme with another equally shameless couple and the same hooting, jeering audience, roaming among them with a microphone a different hostess, white this time but as imperturbable as the first and just as oblivious of everybody's bad manners, even, it seemed to Mrs Ransome, egging them on.

These hostesses (for Mrs Ransome now began to watch regularly) were all much of a muchness, big, bold and, Mrs Ransome thought, with far too much self-confidence (she thought this was what they meant by 'feisty' and would have looked it up in Mr Ransome's dictionary but wasn't sure how it was spelled). They had names that defied gender: Robin, Bobby, Troy and some, like Tiffany, Page and Kirby, that in Mrs Ransome's book weren't names at all.

The presenters and their audience spoke in a language which Mrs Ransome, to begin with anyway, found hard to understand, talking of 'parenting' and 'personal interaction', of 'fine-tuning their sex-lives' and 'taking it up the butt'. It was a language of avowal and exuberant fellowship. 'I hear what you're saying,' they said, smacking each other's hands, 'I know where you're coming from.'

There was Felicia, who wanted long and loving sexual interaction and Dwight, her husband, who just had hungry hands and no marital skills. They both, it was generally agreed, needed to talk, and here in front of this jeering throng, hungry for sensation, was the place they had chosen to do it, finally, as the credits rolled, falling hungrily upon one another, mouth glued to mouth while the audience roared its approval and the presenter looked on with a sadder and wiser smile. 'Thank you people,' she said, and the couple kissed on.

What Mrs Ransome could never get used to was how unabashed the participants were, how unsheepish and how none of these people was ever plain shy. Even when there was a programme about shyness no one who took part was shy in any sense that Mrs Ransome understood it; there was no hanging back and no shortage of unblushing participants willing to stand up and boast of their crippling self-consciousness and the absurdities to which overwhelming diffidence and self-effacingness had brought them. No matter how private or intimate the topic under discussion, none of these eager vociferous people had any shame. On the contrary, they seemed to vie with one another in coming up with confessions of behaviour that grew ever more ingeniously gross and indelicate; one outrageous admission trumped another, the audience greeting each new revelation with wild whoops and yells, hurling advice at the participants and urging them on to retail new depravities.

There were, it's true, rare occasions when some of the audience gave vent not to glee but to outrage, even seeming for a moment, presented with some particularly egregious confession, to be genuinely shocked; but it was only because the presenter, glancing covertly at the audience behind the speaker's back, had pulled a wry face and so cued their affront. The presenter was an accomplice, Mrs Ransome thought, and no better than anyone else, even going out of her way to remind participants of yet more inventive and indelicate acts that they had earlier confided to her in the presumed privacy of the dressing-room. When she jogged their memories they went through an elaborate pantomime of shame (hiding their heads, covering face with hands, shaking with seemingly helpless laughter), all this to indicate that they had never expected such secrets to be made public, let alone retailed to the camera.

Still, Mrs Ransome felt, they were all better than she was. For what none of these whooping, giggling (and often quite obese) creatures seemed in no doubt about was that at the basic level at which these programmes were pitched people were all the same. There was no shame and no reserve and to pretend otherwise was to be stuck up and a hypocrite. Mrs Ransome felt that she was certainly the first and that her husband was probably the second.

The contents of the flat were insured for £50,000. It had originally been much less, but being a solicitor and a careful man besides, Mr Ransome had seen to it that the premium had kept pace with the cost of living. Accordingly this modest agglomeration of household goods, furniture, fixtures and fittings had gone on over the years gently increasing in value; the stereo and the Magimix, the canteen of cutlery, the EPNS salad servers, the tray cloths and tablemats and all the apparatus of that life which the Ransomes had the complete equipment for but had never managed to lead, all this had marched comfortably in step with the index. Durable, sober, unshowy stuff, bought with an eye to use not ornament, hardly diminished by breakage or loss, dutifully dusted and polished over the years so that it was scarcely even abraded by wear or tear – all this had gone uneventfully forward until that terrible night when the column had been ambushed and this ordinary, unpretentious little fraternity seemingly wiped out and what Mrs Ransome modestly called 'our things' had vanished for ever.

So at any rate the insurance company concluded and in due course a cheque arrived for the full value plus an unforeseen increment payable in the absence of any previous claims and which served to cover disruption and compensate for distress.

'The extra is for our trauma,' said Mrs Ransome, looking at the cheque.

'I prefer to call it inconvenience,' Mr Ransome said. 'We've been burgled, not knocked down by a bus. Still, the extra will come in handy.'

He was already working out a scheme for an improved stereo system plus an update on his CD player combined with high definition digital sound and ultra-refinement of tone, all to be fed through a pair of majestic new speakers in hand-crafted mahogany. It would be Mozart as he had never heard him before.

Mrs Ransome was sitting contentedly in a cheap cane rocking-chair she had found a few weeks earlier in a furniture store up the Edgware Road. It was an establishment which, before the burglary, she would never have dreamed of going into, with garish suites, paintings of clowns and, flanking the door, two lifesize pottery leopards. A common shop she would have thought it once, as a bit of her still did, but Mr Anwar had recommended it and sure enough the rocking-chair she'd bought there was wonderfully comfortable and, unlike the easy chair in which she used to sit before the burglary, good for her back. Now that the insurance cheque had come through she planned on getting a matching chair for Mr Ransome, but in the meantime she had bought a rug to put the chair on, and, sewn with a design of an elephant, it glowed under the light from a brass table lamp bought at the same shop. Sitting with what Mr Anwar had told her was an Afghan prayer rug round her shoulders she felt in the middle of the bare sitting-room floor that she was on a cosy and slightly exotic little island.

For the moment Mr Ransome's island was not so cosy, just a chair at the card table on which Mrs Ransome had put the one letter that constituted the day's post. Mr Ransome picked up the envelope. Smelling curry, he said: 'What's for supper?'

'Curry.'

Mr Ransome turned the letter over. It looked like a bill. 'What sort of curry?'

'Lamb,' said Mrs Ransome. 'With apricots. I've been wondering,' she said. 'Would white be too bold?'

'White what?' said Mr Ransome, holding the letter up to the light.

'Well,' she said hesitantly. 'White everything really.'

Mr Ransome did not reply. He was reading the letter.

'You mustn't get too excited,' Mr Ransome said as they were driving towards Aylesbury. 'It could be somebody's sense of humour. Another joke.'

Actually their mood was quite flat and the countryside was flat too; they had scarcely spoken since they had set off, the letter with Mr Ransome's pencilled directions lying on Mrs Ransome's lap.

'Left at the roundabout,' thought Mr Ransome.

'It's left at the roundabout,' Mrs Ransome said.

He had telephoned the storage firm that morning to have a girl answer. It was called Rapid 'n' Reliant Removals 'n' Storage, those 'n's, Mr Ransome thought, a foretaste of trouble; nor was he disappointed.

'Hello. Rapid 'n' Reliant Removals 'n' Storage. Christine Thoseby speaking. How may I help you?'

Mr Ransome asked for Mr Ralston, who had signed the letter.

'At the present time of speaking Mr Ralston is in Cardiff. How may I help you?'

'When will he be back?'

'Not until next week. He's on a tour of our repositories. How may I help you?'

Her repeated promises of help notwithstanding, Christine had the practised lack of interest of someone perpetually painting her nails and when Mr Ransome explained that the previous day he had received a mysterious invoice for £344.36 re the storage of certain household effects, the property of Mr and Mrs Ransome, all Christine said was: 'And?' He began to explain the circumstances but at the suggestion that the effects in question might be stolen property Christine came to life.

'May I interject? I think that's very unlikely, quite frankly, I mean, Rapid 'n' Reliant were established in 1977.'

Mr Ransome tried a different tack. 'You wouldn't happen to know whether any of these household effects you're holding includes some old stereo equipment.'

'Can't help you there, I'm afraid. But if you have any items in storage with Rapid 'n' Reliant they'll show up on the C47, of which you should have a copy. It's a yellow flimsy.'

Mr Ransome started to explain why he didn't have a flimsy but Christine cut him short.

'I wouldn't know that, would I, because I'm in Newport Pagnell? This is the office. The storage depot is in Aylesbury. You can be anywhere nowadays. It's computers. Actually the person who could help you at Aylesbury is Martin but I happen to know he's out on a job most of today.'

'I wonder whether I ought to go down to Aylesbury,' Mr Ransome said, 'just to see if there's anything there.'

Christine was unenthusiastic. 'I can't actually stop you,' she said, 'only they don't have any facilities for visitors. It's not like a kennels,' she added inexplicably.

Mr Ransome having told her the storage firm was in a business park, Mrs Ransome, who was not familiar with the genre, imagined it situated in a setting agreeably pastoral, a park that was indeed a park and attached to some more or less stately home, now sensitively adapted to modern requirements; the estate dotted with workshops possibly; offices nestling discreetly in trees. At the hub of this centre of enterprise she pictured a country house where tall women with folders strode along terraces, typists busied themselves in gilded saloons beneath painted ceilings, a vision which, had she thought to trace it back, she would have found to have derived from those war films where French châteaux taken over by the German High Command bustle with new life on the eve of D-Day.

It was as well she didn't share these romantic expectations with Mr Ransome who, the secretary of several companies and so acquainted with the reality, would have given them short shrift.

It was only when she found herself being driven round a bleak treeless ring-road lined with small factories and surrounded by concrete and rough grass that Mrs Ransome began to revise her expectations.

'It doesn't look very countrified,' Mrs Ransome said.

'Why should it?' said Mr Ransome, about to turn in at some un-Palladian metal gates.

'This is it,' said Mrs Ransome, looking at the letter.

The gates were set in a seven-foot high fence topped with an oblique pelmet of barbed wire so that the place looked less like a park than a prison. Fixed to an empty pillbox was a metal diagram, painted in yellow and blue, showing the whereabouts of the various firms on the estate. Mr Ransome got out to look for Unit 14.

'You are here,' said an arrow, only someone had inserted at the tip of the arrow a pair of crudely drawn buttocks.

Unit 14 appeared to be a few hundred yards inside the perimeter, just about where, had the buttocks been drawn to scale, the navel might have been. Mr Ransome got back in the car and drove slowly on in the gathering dusk until he came to a broad low hangar-like building with double sliding doors, painted red and bare of all identification except for a warning that guard dogs patrolled. There were no other cars and no sign of anybody about.

Mr Ransome pulled at the sliding door, not expecting to find it open. Nor was it.

'It's locked,' said Mrs Ransome.

'You don't say,' Mr Ransome muttered under his breath, and struck out round the side of the building, followed more slowly by Mrs Ransome, picking her way uncertainly over the rubble and clinkers and patches of scrubby grass. Mr Ransome felt his shoe skid on something.

'Mind the dog dirt,' said Mrs Ransome. 'It's all over this grass.' Steps led down to a basement door. Mr Ransome tried this too. It was also locked, a boiler room possibly.

'That looks like a boiler room,' said Mrs Ransome.

He scraped his shoe on the step.

'You'd think they'd make them set an example,' Mrs Ransome said.

'Who?' said Mr Ransome, slurring his polluted shoe over some thin grass.

'The guard dogs.'

They had almost completed a circuit of the hangar when they came on a small frosted window where there was a dim light. It was open an inch or two at the top and was obviously a lavatory, and faintly through the glass Mrs Ransome could see standing on the window-ledge the blurred shape of a toilet roll. It was doubtless a coincidence that it was blue, and forget-me-not blue at that, a shade Mrs Ransome always favoured in her own toilet rolls and which was not always easy to find. She pressed her face to the glass in order to see it more clearly and then saw something else.

'Look, dear,' Mrs Ransome said. But Mr Ransome wasn't looking. He was listening.

'Shut up,' he said. He could hear Mozart.

And floating through the crack of the lavatory window came the full, dark, sumptuous and utterly unmistakable tones of Dame Kiri Te Kanawa.

'Per pietà, ben mio,' she was singing, 'perdona all 'error d'un amante.'

And out it drifted into the damp dusk, rising over Rapid 'n' Reliant at Unit 14 and Croda Adhesives at Unit 16 and Lansyl Selant Applicators plc at Unit 20 (Units 17-19 currently under offer).

'O Dio,' sang Dame Kiri. 'O Dio.'

And the perimeter road heard it and the sheathed and stunted saplings planted there and the dirty dribble of a stream that straggled through a concrete culvert to the lumpy field beyond, where a shabby horse contemplated two barrels and a pole.

Galvanised by the sound of the Antipodean songstress Mr Ransome clambered up the fall pipe and knelt painfully on the window-sill. Clinging to the pipe with one hand he prised open the window an inch or two further and forced his head in as far as it would go, almost slipping off the sill in the process.

'Careful,' said Mrs Ransome.

Mr Ransome began to shout. 'Hello. Hello?'

Mozart stopped and somewhere a bus went by.

In the silence Mr Ransome shouted again, this time almost joyfully. 'Hello!'

Instantly there was bedlam. Dogs burst out barking, a siren went off and Mr and Mrs Ransome were trapped and dazzled by half a dozen security lights focused tightly on their shrinking forms. Petrified, Mr Ransome clung desperately to the lavatory window while Mrs Ransome plastered herself as closely as she could against the wall, one hand creeping (she hoped unobtrusively) up the window-sill to seek the comfort of Mr Ransome's knee.

Then, as suddenly as it had begun, the commotion stopped; the lights went out, the siren trailed off and the barking of the dogs modulated to an occasional growl. Trembling on the sill Mr Ransome heard a door pushed back and unhurried steps walking across the forecourt.

'Sorry about that, people,' said a male voice. 'Burglars, I'm afraid, measures for the detection and discouragement of.'

Mrs Ransome peered into the darkness but still half-blinded by the lights could see nothing. Mr Ransome slithered down the fall pipe to stand beside her and she took his hand.

'This way chaps and chapesses. Over here.'

Mr and Mrs Ransome stumbled across the last of the grass onto the concrete where silhouetted against the open door stood a young man.

Dazed, they followed him into the hangar and in the light they made a sorry-looking pair. Mrs Ransome was limping because one of her heels had broken and she had laddered both her stockings. Mr Ransome had torn the knee of his trousers; there was shit on his shoes and across his forehead where he had pressed his face into the window was a long black smudge.

The young man smiled and put out his hand. 'Maurice. Rosemary. Hi! I'm Martin.'

It was a pleasant open face and though he did have one of those little beards Mrs Ransome thought made them all look like poisoners, for a warehouseman one way and another he looked quite classy. True he was wearing the kind of cap which had once been the distinctive head-gear of American golfers but now seemed of general application, and a little squirt of hair with a rubber band round it coming out of the back, and, again like them all nowadays, his shirt tail was out; still, what gave him a certain air in Mrs Ransome's eyes was his smart maroon cardigan. It was not unlike one she had picked out for Mr Ransome at a Simpson's sale the year before. Loosely knotted around his neck was a yellow silk scarf with horses' heads on it. Mrs Ransome had bought Mr Ransome one of those too, though he had worn it only once as he decided it made him look like a cad. This boy didn't look like a cad; he looked dashing and she thought that if they ever got their belongings back she'd root the scarf out from the wardrobe and make her husband give it another try.

'Follow moi,' said the young man and led them down a cold uncarpeted corridor.

'It's so nice to meet you at long last,' he said over

his shoulder, 'though in the circumstances I feel I know you already.'

'What circumstances?' said Mr Ransome.

'Bear with me one moment,' said Martin.

Mr and Mrs Ransome were left in the dark while the young man fiddled with a lock.

'I'll just illuminate matters a fraction,' he said and a light came on in the room beyond.

'Come in,' said Martin and he laughed.

Tired and dirty and blinking in the light, Mr and Mrs Ransome stumbled through the door and into their own flat.

It was just as they had left it in the evening they had gone to the opera. Here was their carpet, their sofa, their high-backed chairs, the reproduction walnut-veneered coffee table with the scalloped edges and cabriole legs and on it the latest number of the *Gramophone*. Here was Mrs Ransome's embroidery, lying on the end of the sofa where she had put it down before going to change at a quarter to six on that never-to-be-forgotten evening. There on the nest of tables was the glass from which Mr Ransome had had a little drop of something to see him through the first act of *Così*, still (Mrs Ransome touched the rim of the glass with her finger) slightly sticky.

On the mantelpiece the carriage clock, presented to Mr Ransome to mark his 25 years with the firm of Selvey, Ransome, Steele and Co, struck six, though Mrs Ransome was not sure if it was six then or six now. The lights were on, just as they had left them.

'A waste of electricity, I know,' Mr Ransome was wont to say, 'but at least it deters the casual thief,' and on the hall table the evening paper left there by Mr Ransome for Mrs Ransome, who generally read it with her morning coffee the following day.

Other than a cardboard plate with some cold half-eaten curry which Martin neatly heeled under the sofa, mouthing 'Sorry', everything, every little thing was exactly as it should be; they might have been at home in their flat in Naseby Mansions, St John's Wood and not in a hangar on an industrial estate on the outskirts of nowhere.

Gone was the feeling of foreboding with which Mrs Ransome had set out that afternoon; now there was only joy as she wandered round the room, occasionally picking up some cherished object with a smile and an 'Oh!' of reacquaintance, sometimes holding it up for her husband to see.

For his part Mr Ransome was almost moved, particularly when he spotted his old CD player, his trusty old CD player as he was inclined to think of it now, not quite up to the mark, it's true, the venerable old thing, but still honest and old-fashioned; yes, it was good to see it again and he gave Mrs Ransome a brief blast of *Così*.

Watching this reunion with a smile almost of pride, Martin said: 'Everything in order? I tried to keep it all just as it was.'

'Oh yes,' said Mrs Ransome, 'it's perfect.'

'Astonishing,' said her husband.

Mrs Ransome remembered something. 'I'd put a casserole in the oven.'

'Yes,' said Martin, 'I enjoyed that.'

'It wasn't dry?' said Mrs Ransome.

'Only a touch,' said Martin, following them into the bedroom. 'It would perhaps have been better at Gas Mark 3.'

Mrs Ransome nodded and noticed on the dressing-table the piece of kitchen paper (she remembered how they had run out of Kleenex) with which she had blotted her lipstick three months before.

'Kitchen,' said Martin as if they might not know the way, though it was exactly where it should have been, and exactly how too, except that the casserole dish, now empty, stood washed and waiting on the draining-board.

'I wasn't sure where that went,' said Martin apologetically.

'That's all right', said Mrs Ransome, 'it lives in here.' She opened the cupboard by the sink and popped the dish away.

'That was my guess,' said Martin, 'though I didn't like to risk it.' He laughed and Mrs Ransome laughed too.

Mr Ransome scowled. The young man was civil enough, if over-familiar, but it all seemed a bit too relaxed. A crime had been committed after all, and not a petty one either; this was stolen property; what was it doing here?

Mr Ransome thought it was time to take charge of the situation.

'Tea?' said Martin.

'No thank you,' said Mr Ransome.

'Yes please,' said his wife.

'Then,' said Martin, 'we need to talk.'

Mrs Ransome had never heard the phrase used in real life as it were and she looked at this young man with new-found recognition: she knew where he was coming from. So did Mr Ransome.

'Yes, indeed,' said Mr Ransome, decisively, sitting down at the kitchen table and meaning to kick off by asking this altogether too pleased with himself young man, what this was all about.

'Perhaps,' said Martin, giving Mrs Ransome her tea, 'perhaps you would like to tell me what this is all about. I mean with all due respect, as they say.'

This was too much for Mr Ransome.

'Perhaps,' he exploded, 'and with all due respect, you'd like to tell me why it is you're wearing my cardigan.'

'You never wore it much,' said Mrs Ransome placidly. 'Lovely tea.'

'That isn't the point, Rosemary.' Mr Ransome seldom used her Christian name except as a form of blunt instrument. 'And that's my silk scarf.'

'You never wore that at all. You said it made you look like a cad.'

'That's why I like it,' said Martin, happily, 'the cad factor. However all good things come to an end, as they say.' And unhurriedly (and quite unrepentantly, thought Mr Ransome) he took off the cardigan, unknotted the scarf and laid them both on the table.

Pruned of these sheltering encumbrances, Martin's T-shirt, the message of which had hitherto only been hinted at, now fearlessly proclaimed itself, 'Got a stiffy? Wear a Jiffy!' and in brackets 'drawing on back'. As Mr Ransome eased forward in his chair in order to shield his wife from the offending illustration, Mrs Ransome slightly eased back.

'Actually,' said Martin, 'we've worn one or two of your things. I started off with your brown overcoat which I just tried on originally as a bit of a joke.'

'A joke?' said Mr Ransome, the humorous qualities of that particular garment never having occurred to him.

'Yes. Only now I've grown quite fond of it. It's great.'

'But it must be too big for you,' said Mrs Ransome.

'I know. That's why it's so great. And you've got tons of scarves. Cleo thinks you've got really good taste.'

'Cleo?' said Mrs Ransome.

'My partner.'

Then, catching sight of Mr Ransome by now

pop-eyed with fury, Martin shrugged. 'After all, it was you who gave us the green light.' He went into the sitting-room and came back with a folder, which he laid on the kitchen table.

'Just tell me,' said Mr Ransome with terrible calmness, 'why it is our things are here.'

So Martin explained. Except it wasn't really an explanation and when he'd finished they weren't much further on.

He had come in to work one morning about three months ago ('February 15,' Mrs Ransome supplied helpfully) and unlocking the doors had found their flat set out just as it had been in Naseby Mansions and just as they saw it now — carpets down, lights on, warm, a smell of cooking from the kitchen.

'I mean,' said Martin happily, '*home.*'

'But surely,' Mr Ransome said, 'you must have realised that this was, to say the least, unusual?'

'Very unusual,' said Martin. Normally, he said, home contents were containered, crated and sealed, and the container parked in the back lot until required. 'We store loads of furniture, but I might go for six months and never see an armchair.'

'But why were they all dumped here?' said Mrs Ransome.

'Dumped?' said Martin, 'you call this dumped? It's beautiful, it's a poem.'

'Why?' said Mr Ransome.

'Well, when I came in that morning, there was an envelope on the hall table . . .'

'That's where I put the letters normally,' said Mrs Ransome.

'. . . an envelope,' said Martin, 'containing £3000 in cash to cover storage costs for two months, well clear of our normal charges I can tell you. And,' said Martin, taking a card out of the folder, 'there was this.'

It was a sheet torn from the *Delia Smith Cookery Calendar* with a recipe for the hotpot which Mrs Ransome had made that afternoon and which she had left in the oven. On the back of it was written: 'Leave exactly as it is,' then in brackets, 'but feel free to use.' This was underlined.

'So, where your overcoat was concerned and the scarves etc, I felt,' Martin searched for the right word, 'I felt that that was my *imprimatur*.' (He had been briefly at the University of Warwick.)

'But anybody could have written that,' Mr Ransome said.

'And leave £3000 in cash with it?' said Martin. 'No fear. Only I did check. Newport Pagnell knew nothing about it. Cardiff. Leeds. I had it run through the computer and they drew a complete blank. So I thought: "Well, Martin, the stuff's here. For the time being it's paid for, so why not just make yourself at home?" So I did. I could have done with the choice of CDs being a bit more eclectic, though. My guess is you're a Mozart fan?'

'I still think,' said Mr Ransome testily, 'you might have made more enquiries before making so free with our belongings.'

'It's not usual, I agree,' said Martin, 'only why should I? I'd no reason to . . . smell a rat?'

Mr Ransome took in (and was irritated by) these occasional notes of inappropriate interrogation with which Martin (and the young generally) seemed often to end a sentence. He had heard it in the mouth of the office boy without realising it had got as far as Aylesbury ('And where are you going now, Foster?' 'For my lunch?'). It seemed insolent, though it was hard to say why and it invariably put Mr Ransome in a bad temper (which was why Foster did it).

Martin on the other hand seemed unconscious of the irritation he was causing, his serenity so impervious Mr Ransome put it down to drugs. Now he sat happily at the kitchen table and while Mr Ransome fussed round the flat on the look-out for evidence of damage or dilapidation or even undue wear and tear, Martin chatted comfortably to Rosemary, as he called her.

'He just needs to lighten up a bit,' said Martin as Mr Ransome banged about in the cupboards.

Mrs Ransome wasn't sure if lighten up was the same as brighten up but catching his drift smiled and nodded.

'It's been like playing houses,' said Martin, 'Cleo and I live over a dry-cleaners normally.'

Mrs Ransome thought Cleo might be black but she didn't like to ask.

'Actually,' and Martin dropped his voice because Mr Ransome was in the pantry cupboard counting the bottles of wine in the rack, 'actually it's perked things up between us two. Change of scene, you know what they say.'

Mrs Ransome nodded knowledgeably; it was a topic frequently touched on in the afternoon programmes.

'Good bed,' whispered Martin, 'the mattress give you lots of — what's the word? — purchase.' Martin gave a little thrust with his hips. 'Know what I mean, Rosemary?' He winked.

'It's orthopaedic,' Mrs Ransome said hastily. 'Mr Ransome has a bad back.'

'I'd probably have one too if I'd lived here much longer.' Martin patted her hand. 'Only joking.'

'What I don't understand,' said Mr Ransome, coming into the kitchen while Martin still had his hand over his wife's (Mr Ransome didn't understand that either), 'what I don't understand is how whoever it was transported our things here could remember so exactly where everything went.'

'Trouble ye no more,' said Martin and he went out into the hall and brought back a photograph album. It was a present Mr Ransome had bought Mrs Ransome when he was urging her to find a hobby. He had also bought her a camera which she had never managed to fathom so that the camera never got used, nor did the album. Except that now it was full of photographs.

'The polaroid camera,' Martin said, 'the blessings thereof.'

There were a dozen or so photographs for every

room in the flat on the night in question; general views of the room, corners of the room, a close-up of the mantelpiece, another of the desk-top, every room and every surface recorded in conscientious detail, much as if, had her flat been the setting for a film, the continuity assistant would have recorded them.

'And our name and address?' Mr Ransome said.

'Simple,' said Martin. 'Open . . .'

'Any drawer,' said he and Mrs Ransome together.

'All these photographs,' Mrs Ransome said. 'Whoever they are, they must have no end of money. Don't they make it look nice.'

'It is nice,' said Martin. 'We're going to miss it.'

'It's not only that all our things are in the right place,' Mr Ransome said, 'The rooms are in the right place too.'

'Screens,' said Martin. 'They must have brought screens with them.'

'There's no ceiling,' said Mr Ransome triumphantly. 'They didn't manage that.'

'They managed the chandelier,' said his wife. And so they had, suspending it from a handy beam.

'Well I don't think we need to prolong this stage

of the proceedings any longer than we have to,' said Mr Ransome. 'I'll contact my insurance company and tell them our belongings have been found. They will then doubtless contact you over their collection and return. There doesn't seem to be anything missing but at this stage one can't be sure.'

'Oh, there's nothing missing,' said Martin. 'One or two After Eights perhaps, but I can easily replenish those.'

'No, no,' said Mrs Ransome, 'that won't be necessary. They're . . .' and she smiled, 'they're on the house.'

Mr Ransome frowned and when Martin went off to find the various pro-formas he whispered to Mrs Ransome that they would have to have everything cleaned.

'I don't like to think what's been going on. There was a bit of kitchen paper on your dressing-table with what was almost certainly blood. And I've a feeling they may have been sleeping in our bed.'

'We'll exchange flimsies,' said Martin. 'One flimsy for you. One flimsy for me. Your effects. Do you say "effects" when a person's still around? Or is it just when they're dead?'

'Dead,' said Mr Ransome authoritatively. 'In this case it's property.'

'Effects,' said Martin. 'Good word.'

Standing on the forecourt as they were going Martin kissed Mrs Ransome on both cheeks. He was about the age their son would have been, Mrs Ransome thought, had they had a son.

'I feel like I'm one of the family,' he said.

'Yes,' thought Mr Ransome; if they'd had a son this is what it would have been like. Irritating, perplexing. Feeling got at. They wouldn't have been able to call their lives their own.

Mr Ransome managed to shake hands.

'All's well that ends well,' said Martin, and patted his shoulder. 'Take care.'

'How do we know he wasn't in on it?' said Mr Ransome in the car.

'He doesn't look the type,' said Mrs Ransome.

'Oh? What type is that? Have you ever come across a case like this before? Have you ever heard of it? What type does it take, that's what I'd like to know?'

'We're going a little fast,' said Mrs Ransome.

'I shall have to inform the police, of course,' Mr

Ransome said.

'They weren't interested before so they'll be even less interested now.'

'Who are you?'

'Beg pardon?'

'I'm the solicitor. Who are you? Are you the expert?'

They drove in silence for a while.

'Of course, I shall want some compensation. The distress. The agony of mind. The inconvenience. They're all quantifiable, and must be taken into account in the final settlement.'

He was already writing the letter in his head.

In due course, the contents of the flat came back to Naseby Mansions, a card pinned to one of the crates saying. 'Feel Free to Use. Martin.' And, in brackets, 'Joke'. Mr Ransome insisted that everything must be put back just as it had been before, which might have proved difficult had it not been for the aide-mémoire in the form of Mrs Ransome's photograph album. Even so the gang who returned the furniture were less meticulous than the burglars who had removed it, besides being much slower. Still, the flat having been decorated throughout and the covers washed, hoovered or dry-cleaned, the place gradually came to look much as it had done before and life returned to what Mrs Ransome used to think of as normal but didn't now, quite.

Quite early on in the proceedings, and while Mr Ransome was at the office, Mrs Ransome tried out her cane rocking-chair and rug in the now much less spartan conditions of the lounge, but though the chair was as comfortable as ever the ensemble didn't look right and made her feel she was sitting in a department store. So she relegated the chair to the spare room where from time to time she visited it and sat reviewing her life. But no, it was not the same and eventually she put the chair out for the caretaker who incorporated it into his scheme of things in the room behind the boiler, where he was now trying to discover the books of Jane Austen.

Mr Ransome fared better than his wife, for although he had had to reimburse the insurance company over their original cheque he was able to claim that having already ordered some new speakers (he hadn't) this should be taken into account and allowance made, which it duly was, thus enabling him to invest in some genuinely state of the art equipment.

From time to time over the next few months traces of Martin and Cleo's brief occupation would surface – a contraceptive packet (empty) that had been thrust under the mattress, a handkerchief down the side of the settee and, in one of the mantelpiece ornaments, a lump of hard brown material wrapped in silver paper. Tentatively Mrs Ransome sniffed it, then donned her Marigold gloves and put it down the lavatory, assuming that was where it belonged, though it was only after several goes that it was reluctantly flushed, Mrs Ransome sitting meanwhile on the side of the bath, waiting for the cistern to refill, and wondering how it came to be on the mantelpiece in the first place. A joke possibly, though not one she shared with Mr Ransome.

Strange hairs were another item that put in regular appearances, long fair ones which were obviously Martin's, darker crinklier ones she supposed must be Cleo's. The incidence of these hairs wasn't split evenly between Mr and Mrs Ransome's respective wardrobes; indeed, since Mr Ransome didn't complain about them, she presumed he never found any, as he would certainly have let her know if he had.

She, on the other hand, found them everywhere – among her dresses, her coats, her underwear, his hairs as well as hers, and little ones as well as long ones, so that she was left puzzling over what it was they could have been up to that wasn't constrained by the normal boundaries of gender and propriety. Had Martin worn her knickers on his head, she wondered (in one pair there were three hairs); had the elastic on her brassière always been as loose as it was now (two hairs there, one fair, one dark)?

Still, sitting opposite Mr Ransome in his earphones of an evening, she could contemplate with equanimity, and even a small thrill, that she had shared her underclothes with a third party. Or two third parties possibly. 'You don't mean a third party,' Mr Ransome would have said, but this was another argument for keeping quiet.

There was one reminder of the recent past, though, that they were forced to share, if only by accident. They had had their supper one Saturday evening after which Mr Ransome was planning to record a live broadcast of *Il Seraglio* on Radio 3. Mrs Ransome, reflecting that there was never anything on TV worth watching on a Saturday night, had settled down to read a novel about some lacklustre in-fidelities in a Cotswold setting while Mr Ransome prepared to record. He had put in a tape that he thought was blank but checking it on the machine was startled to find that it began with a peal of help-less laughter. Mrs Ransome looked up. Mr Ransome listened long enough to detect that there were two people laughing, a man and a woman and since they showed no sign of stopping was about to switch it off when Mrs Ransome said: 'No, Maurice. Leave it. This might be a clue.'

So they listened in silence as the laughter went on, almost uninterrupted, until after three or four minutes it began to slacken and break up and who-ever it was who was still laughing was left panting and breathless, this breathlessness gradually mod-ulating into another sound, the second subject as it were, a groan and then a cry leading to a rhythmic pumping as stern and as purposeful as the other had been silly and light-hearted. At one point the microphone was moved closer to catch a sound that was so moist and wet it hardly seemed human.

'It sounds,' said Mrs Ransome, 'like custard boiling,' though she knew that it wasn't. Making custard must seldom be so effortful as this seemed to be, nor is the custard urged on with affirmative yells, nor do the cooks cry out when, in due course, the custard starts to boil over.

'I don't think we want to listen to this, do we?' Mr Ransome said and switched over to Radio 3, where they came in on the reverent hush that preceded the arrival of Claudio Abbado.

Later when they were in bed Mrs Ransome said: 'I suppose we'd better return that tape?'

'What for?' said Mr Ransome, 'the tape is mine. In any case, we can't. It's wiped. I recorded over it.'

This was a lie. Mr Ransome had wanted to record over it, it's true, but felt that whenever he listened to the music he would remember what lay underneath and this would put paid to any possible sublimity. So he had put the tape in the kitchen bin. Then, thinking about it as Mrs Ransome was in the bathroom brushing her teeth, he went and delved among the potato peelings and old teabags, and, picking off a tomato skin that had stuck to it, he hid the cassette in the bookcase behind a copy of *Salmon on Torts*, a hidey hole where he also kept a cache of photographs of some suburban sexual acts, the legacy of a messy divorce case in Epsom that he had conducted a few years before. The bookcase had, of course, gone to Aylesbury along with everything else but had been returned intact, the hiding place seemingly undetected by Martin.

Actually it had not been undetected at all: the photographs had been what he and Cleo had been laughing about on the tape in the first place.

Not a secret from Martin, nor were the snaps a secret from Mrs Ransome who, idly looking at the bookcase one afternoon and wondering what to cook for supper, had seen the title *Salmon on Torts* and thought it had a vaguely culinary sound to it. She had put the photographs back undisturbed but every few months or so would check to see that they were still there. When they were she felt somehow reassured.

So sometimes now when Mr Ransome sat in his chair with his earphones on listening to *Magic Flute* it was not *Magic Flute* he was listening to at all. Gazing abstractedly at his reading wife his ears were full of Martin and Cleo moaning and crying and taking it out on one another again and again and again. No matter how often he listened to the tape Mr Ransome never ceased to be amazed by it; that two human beings could give themselves up so utterly and unreservedly to one another and to the moment was beyond his comprehension; it seemed to him miraculous.

Listening to the tape so often he became every bit as familiar with it as with something by Mozart. He came to recognise Martin's long intake of breath as marking the end of a mysterious bridging passage (Cleo was actually on hand and knees, Martin behind her) when the languorous andante (little mewings from the girl) accelerated into the percussive allegro assai (hoarse cries from them both) which in its turn gave way to an even more frantic coda, a sudden rallentando ('No, no, not yet,' she was crying, then 'Yes, yes, yes') followed by panting, sighing, silence and finally sleep. Not an imaginative man, Mr Ransome nevertheless found himself thinking that if one built up a library of such tapes it would be possible to bestow on them the sexual equivalent of Köchel numbers, even trace the development of some sort of style in sexual intercourse, with early, middle and late periods, the whole apparatus of Mozartean musicology adapted to these new and thwacking rhythms.

Such were Mr Ransome's thoughts as he sat across from his wife, who was having another stab at Barbara Pym. She knew he wasn't listening to

Mozart though there were few obvious signs and nothing so vulgar as a bulge in his trousers. No, there was just a look of strain on Mr Ransome's face, which was the very opposite of the look he had when he was listening to his favourite composer; an intensity of attention and a sense that, were he to listen hard enough, he might hear something on the tape he had previously missed.

Mrs Ransome would listen to the tape herself from time to time but lacking the convenient camouflage of Mozart she confined her listening experiences to the afternoons. Getting out her folding household steps she would pull down *Salmon on Torts* then reach in behind it for the tape (the photographs seemed as silly and laughable to her as they had to Martin and Cleo). Then, having poured herself a small sherry, she would settle down to listen to them making love, marvelling still after at least a dozen hearings at the length and persistence of the process and its violent and indecorous outcome. Afterwards she would go and lie on the bed, reflecting that this was the same bed on which it had all happened and think again about it happening.

These discreet (and discrete) epiphanies apart,

life after they had recovered their possessions went on much the same as it had before they lost them. Sometimes, though, lying there on the bed or waiting to get up in the morning, Mrs Ransome would get depressed, feeling she had missed the bus; though what bus it was or where it was headed she would have found it hard to say. Prior to the visit to Aylesbury and the return of their things, she had, she thought, persuaded herself that the burglary had been an opportunity, with each day bringing its crop of small adventures – a visit from Dusty, a walk down to Mr Anwar's, a trip up the Edgware Road. Now, re-ensconced among her possessions, Mrs Ransome feared that her diversions were at an end; life had returned to normal but it was a normal she no longer relished or was contented with.

The afternoons particularly were dull and full of regret. It's true she continued to watch the television, no longer so surprised at what people got up to as she once had been but even (as with Martin and Cleo) mildly envious. She grew so accustomed to the forms of television discourse that she occasionally let slip a tell-tale phrase herself, remarking once, for instance, that there had been a bit of hassle on the 74 bus.

'Hassle?' said Mr Ransome. 'Where did you pick up that expression?'

'Why?' said Mrs Ransome innocently. 'Isn't it a proper word?'

'Not in my vocabulary.'

It occurred to Mrs Ransome that this was the time for counselling; previously an option it had now become a necessity so she tried to reach Dusty via her Helpline.

'I'm sorry but Ms Briscoe is not available to take your call,' said a recorded voice, which was immediately interrupted by a real presence.

'Hello. Mandy speaking. How may I help you?'

Mrs Ransome explained that she needed to talk to somebody about the sudden return of all the stolen property. 'I have complicated feelings about it,' said Mrs Ransome and tried to explain.

Mandy was doubtful. 'It might come under post-traumatic stress syndrome,' she said, 'only I wouldn't bank on it. They're clamping down on that now we're coming to the end of this year's financial year, and anyway it's meant for rape and murder and whatnot, whereas we've had people ringing up who've just had a bad time at the dentist's. You don't feel the furniture's dirty, do you?'

'No,' said Mrs Ransome. 'We've had everything cleaned anyway.'

'Well, if you've kept the receipts I could ring Bickerton Road and get them to give you something back.'

'Never mind,' said Mrs Ransome, 'I expect I shall cope.'

'Well, it's what we all have to do in the end, isn't it,' said Mandy.

'What's that?' said Mrs Ransome.

'Cope, dear. After all, that's the name of the game. And the way you've described it,' Mandy said, 'it seems a very *caring* burglary.'

Mandy was right, though it was the caringness that was the problem. Had this been a burglary in the ordinary way it would have been easier to get over. Even the comprehensive removal of everything they had in the world was something Mrs Ransome could have adjusted to; been 'positive' about, even enjoyed. But it was the wholesale disappearance coupled with the meticulous reconstruction and return that rankled. Who would want to rob them to that degree and having robbed them would choose to make such immaculate reparations? It seemed to Mrs Ransome that she had been robbed twice over, by the loss, first, of her possessions, then of the chance to transcend that loss. It was not fair, nor did it make sense; she thought perhaps this was what they meant when they talked about 'losing the plot'.

People seldom wrote to the Ransomes. They had the occasional card from Canada where Mr Ransome had some relatives of his mother who dutifully kept up the connection; Mrs Ransome would write back, her card as flavourless as theirs, the message from Canada little more than 'Hello. We are still here,' and her reply, 'Yes, and so are we.' Generally, though, the post consisted of bills and business communications and picking them up from the box downstairs in the lobby Mrs Ransome scarcely bothered to look them through, putting them unsifted on the hall table where Mr Ransome would deal with them before he had his supper. On this particular morning she'd just completed this ritual when she noticed that the letter on top was from South America, and that it was not addressed to Mr M. Ransome but to a Mr M. Hanson. This had happened once before, Mr Ransome putting the misdirected letter in the caretaker's box with a note asking him or the postman to be more careful in future.

Less tolerant of her husband's fussing than she once had been, Mrs Ransome didn't want this performance again so she put the letter on one side so that after her lunch she could go up to the eighth floor, find Mr Hanson's door and slip it underneath. At least it would be an outing.

It was several years since she had been up to the top of the Mansions. There had been some alterations, she knew, as Mr Ransome had had to write a letter of complaint to the landlords about the noise of the workmen and the dirt in the lift; but, as tenants came and went, someone was always having something done somewhere and Mrs Ransome came to take renovation as a fact of life. Still, venturing out of the lift she was surprised how airy it all was now; it might have been a modern building so light and unshadowed and spacious was the landing. Unlike their dark and battered mahogany, this woodwork had been stripped and bleached and whereas their hallway was covered in stained and pockmarked orange floor-covering, this had a thick smoky blue fitted carpet that lapped the walls and muffled every sound. Above was a high octagonal skylight and beneath it an octagonal sofa to match. It looked less like the hallway of a block of mansion flats than a hotel or one of the new hospitals. Nor was it simply the decoration that had changed. Mrs Ransome remembered there being several flats but now there seemed to be only one, no trace of the other doors remaining. She looked for a name on this one door just to be sure but there was no name and no letter-box. She bent down intending to slip the letter from South America underneath but the carpet was so thick that this was difficult and it wouldn't go. Above Mrs Ransome's head and unseen by her, a security camera, which she had taken for a light fitting, moved round like some clumsy reptile in a series of silent jerks until it had her in frame. She was trying to press the pile of the carpet down when there was a faint buzz and the door swung silently open.

'Come in,' said a disembodied voice and holding up the letter as if it were an invitation Mrs Ransome went in.

There was no one in the hall and she waited uncertainly, smiling helpfully in case someone was watching. The hall was identical in shape to theirs but twice the size and done up like the lobby in the same blond wood and faintly stippled walls. They must have knocked through, she thought, taken in the flat next door, taken in all the flats probably, the whole of the top floor one flat.

'I brought a letter,' she said, more loudly than if there had been someone there. 'It came by mistake.'

There was no sound.

'I think it's from South America. Peru. That is if the name's Hanson. Anyway,' she said desperately, 'I'll just put it down then go.'

She was about to put the letter down on a cube of transparent perspex that she took to be a table when she heard behind her an exhausted sigh and turned to find that the door had closed. But as the door behind her closed so, with a mild intake of breath, the door in front of her opened, and through it she saw another doorway, this one with a bar across the top, and suspended from the bar a young man.

He was pulling himself up to the bar seemingly without much effort, and saying his score out loud. He was wearing grey track suit bottoms and earphones and that was all. He had reached 11. Mrs Ransome waited, still holding up the letter and not quite sure where to look. It was a long time since she had been so close to someone so young and so naked, the trousers slipping down low over his hips so that she could see the thin line of blond hair climbing the flat belly to his navel. He was tiring now and the last two pull-ups, 19 and 20, cost him great effort and after he had almost shouted '20' he stood there panting, one hand still grasping the bar, the earphones low round his neck. There was a faint graze of hair under his arms and some just beginning on his chest and like Martin he had the same squirt of hair at the back though his was longer and twisted into a knot.

Mrs Ransome thought she had never seen anyone so beautiful in all her life.

'I brought a letter,' she began again. 'It came by mistake.'

She held it out to him but he made no move to take it, so she looked round for somewhere to put it down.

There was a long refectory table down the middle of the room and by the wall a sofa that was nearly as long, but these were the only objects in the room that Mrs Ransome would have called proper furniture. There were some brightly coloured plastic cubes scattered about which she supposed might serve as occasional tables, or possibly stools. There was a tall steel pyramid with vents which seemed to be a standard lamp. There was an old-fashioned pram with white-walled tyres and huge curved springs. On one wall was a dray-horse collar and on another a cavalier's hat and next to it a huge blown-up photograph of Lana Turner.

'She was a film star,' the young man said. 'It's an original.'

'Yes, I remember,' Mrs Ransome said.

'Why, did you know her?'

'Oh no,' Mrs Ransome said. 'Anyway, she was American.'

The floor was covered in a thick white carpet which she imagined would show every mark though there were no marks that she could see. Still, it didn't seem to Mrs Ransome to add up, this room, and with one of the walls glass, giving out on to a terrace, it felt less like a room than an unfinished window display in a department store, a bolt of tweed flung casually across the table what it needed somehow to make sense.

He saw her looking.

'It's been in magazines,' he said. 'Sit down,' and he took the letter from her.

He sat at one end of the sofa and she sat at the other. He put his feet up and if she had put her feet up too there would still have been plenty of room between them. He looked at the letter, turning it over once or twice without opening it.

'It's from Peru,' Mrs Ransome said.

'Yes,' he said, 'thanks,' and tore it in two.

'It might be important,' said Mrs Ransome.

'It's always important,' said the young man, and dropped the pieces on the carpet.

Mrs Ransome looked at his feet. Like every bit of him that she could see they were perfect, the toes not bent up and useless like her own, or Mr Ransome's. These were long, square-cut and even expressive; they looked as if at a pinch they could deputise for the hands and even play a musical instrument.

'I've never seen you in the lift,' she said.

'I have a key. Then it doesn't have to stop at the other floors.' He smiled. 'It's handy.'

'Not for us,' said Mrs Ransome.

'That's true,' and he laughed, unoffended. 'Anyway, I pay extra.'

'I didn't know you could do that,' said Mrs Ransome.

'You can't,' he said.

Mrs Ransome had an idea he was a singer, but felt that if she asked he might cease to treat her as an equal. She also wondered if he was on drugs. Silence certainly didn't seem to bother him and he lay back at his end of the sofa, smiling and completely at ease.

'I should go,' said Mrs Ransome.

'Why?'

He felt in his armpit then waved an arm at the room.

'This is all her.'

'Who?'

He indicated the torn-up letter. 'She did the place up. She's an interior decorator. Or was. She now ranches in Peru.'

'Cattle?' said Mrs Ransome.

'Horses.'

'Oh,' said Mrs Ransome. 'That's nice. There can't be too many people who've done that.'

'Done what?'

'Been an interior decorator then . . . then . . . looked after horses.'

He considered this. 'No. Though she was like that. You know, sporadic.' He surveyed the room.

'Do you like it?'

'Well,' said Mrs Ransome, 'it's a little strange. But I like the space.'

'Yes, it's a great space. A brilliant space.'

Mrs Ransome hadn't quite meant that but she was not unfamiliar with the concept of space as they talked about space a lot in the afternoons, how people needed it, how they had to be given it and how it had not to be trespassed on.

'She did the place up,' he said, 'then of course she moved in.'

'So you felt,' said Mrs Ransome (and the phrase might have been her first faltering steps in Urdu it seemed so strange on her lips), 'you felt that she had invaded your space.'

He pointed one beautiful foot at her in affirmation.

'She did. She did. I mean take that fucking pram . . .'

'I remember those,' said Mrs Ransome.

'Yes, well, sure, only *apparently*,' he said, 'though it wasn't apparent to me, that is not there as a pram. It is there as an object. And it had to be just on that fucking spot. And because I, like, happened to move it, like half an inch, madam went ballistic. Threatened to take everything away. Leave the place bare. As if I cared. Anyway, she's history.'

Since she was in Peru Mrs Ransome felt that she was geography too, a bit, but she didn't say so. Instead she nodded and said: 'Men have different needs.'

'You're right.'

'Are you hurting?' Mrs Ransome said.

'I was hurting,' the young man said, 'only now I'm stepping back from it. I think you have to.'

Mrs Ransome nodded sagely.

'Was she upset?' she asked, and she longed to take hold of his foot.

'Listen,' he said, 'this woman was always upset.' He stared out of the window.

'When did she leave you?'

'I don't know. I lose track of time. Three months, four months ago.'

'Like February?' said Mrs Ransome. And it wasn't a question.

'Right.'

'Hanson, Ransome,' she said. 'They're not really alike but I suppose if you're from Peru . . .'

He didn't understand, as why should he, so she told him, told him the whole story, beginning with them coming back from the opera, and the police and the trek out to Aylesbury, the whole tale.

When she'd finished, he said: 'Yeah, that sounds like Paloma. It's the kind of thing she would do. She had a funny sense of humour. That's South America for you.'

Mrs Ransome nodded, as if any gaps in this account of events could be put down to the region and the well-known volatility of its inhabitants; the spell of the pampas, the length of the Amazon, llamas, piranha fish – compared with phenomena like these what was a mere burglary in North London? Still, one question nagged.

'Who'd she have got to do it with such care?' Mrs Ransome asked.

'Oh, that's easy. Roadies.'

'Roadies?' said Mrs Ransome. 'Do you mean navvies?'

'A stage crew. Guys who do set-ups. Picked the lock. Took the photographs. Dismantled your set up, put it up again in Aylesbury. Designer job probably. They're doing it all the time one way or another. No problem, nothing too much trouble . . . provided you pay extra.' He winked. 'Anyway,' and he looked round the sparsely-furnished room, 'it wouldn't be such a big job. Is your place like this?'

'Not exactly,' Mrs Ransome said. 'Ours is . . . well . . . more complicated.'

He shrugged. 'She could pay. She was rich. Anyway,' he said, getting up from the sofa and taking her hand, 'I'm sorry you've been inconvenienced on my account.'

'No,' said Mrs Ransome. 'It was well, you know, kind of weird to begin with but I've tried to be positive about it. And I think I've grown, you know.'

They were standing by the pram.

'We had one of these once,' Mrs Ransome said. 'Briefly.' It was something she had not spoken of for thirty years.

'A baby?'

'He was going to be called Donald,' Mrs Ransome said, 'but he never got that far.'

Unaware that a revelation had been made the young man stroked his nipple reflectively as he walked her out into the hall.

'Thank you for clearing up the mystery,' she said and (the boldest thing she had ever done in her life) touched him lightly on his bare hip. She was prepared for him to flinch but he didn't, nor was there any change in his demeanour, which was still smiling and relaxed. Except that he also must have thought something out of the ordinary was called for because, taking her hand, he raised it to his lips and kissed it.

One afternoon a few weeks later Mrs Ransome was coming into Naseby Mansions with her shopping when she saw a van outside and crossing the downstairs lobby she met a young man with a cavalier's hat on and wearing a horse collar round his neck. He was pushing a pram.

'Is he going?' she asked the young man.

'Yeah.' He leaned on the pram. 'Again.'

'Does he move often?'

'Look, lady. This guy moves house the way other people move their bowels. All this' – and he indicated the pram, the horse collar and the cavalier's hat – 'is getting the elbow. We're going Chinese now, apparently.'

'Let me help you with that,' Mrs Ransome said, taking the pram as he struggled to get it through the door. She wheeled it down the ramp, rocking it slightly as she waited while he disposed the other items inside the van.

'A bit since you pushed one of those,' he said as he took it off her. She perched with her shopping on the wall by the entrance, watching as he packed blankets round the furniture, wondering if he was one of the roadies who had moved them. She had not told Mr Ransome how the burglary had come to pass. It was partly because he would have made a fuss, would have insisted on going up to the top floor to have a word with the young man personally. ('Probably in on it too,' he would have said.) It was a meeting Mrs Ransome had not been able to contemplate without embarrassment. As the van drove off she waved, then went upstairs.

End of story, or so Mrs Ransome thought, except that one Sunday afternoon a couple of months later Mr Ransome suffered a stroke. Mrs Ransome was in the kitchen stacking the dishwasher and hearing a bump went in and found her husband lying on the floor in front of the bookcase, a cassette in one hand, a dirty photograph in the other, and Salmon on Torts open on the floor. Mr Ransome was conscious but could neither speak nor move.

Mrs Ransome did all the right things, placing a cushion under his head and a rug over his body before ringing the ambulance. She hoped that even in his stricken state her efficiency and self-possession would impress her prostrate husband, but looking down at him while she was waiting to be connected to the appropriate service, she saw in his eyes no sign of approval or gratitude, just a look of sheer terror.

Powerless to draw his wife's attention to the cassette clutched in his hand, or even to relinquish it, her helpless husband watched as Mrs Ransome briskly collected up the photographs, something at the very back of his mind registering how little interest or surprise was occasioned by this tired old smut. Lastly (the klaxon of the ambulance already audible as it raced by the park) she knelt beside him and prised the cassette free of his waxen fingers before popping it matter of factly into her apron pocket. She held his hand for a second (still bent to the shape of the offending cassette) and thought that perhaps the look in his eyes was now no longer terror but had turned to shame; so she smiled and squeezed his hand, saying, 'It's not important,' at which point the ambulance men rang the bell.

Mr Ransome has not come well out of this narrative; seemingly impervious to events he has, unlike his wife, neither changed nor grown in stature. Owning a dog might have shown him in a better light, but handy though Naseby Mansions was for the park, to be cooped up in a flat is no life for a dog; a hobby would have helped, a hobby other than Mozart, that is, the quest for the perfect performance only serving to emphasise Mr Ransome's punctiliousness and general want of warmth. No, to learn to take things as they come he would have been better employed in the untidier arts, photography, say, or painting watercolours; a family would have been untidy too, and, though it seems it was only Mrs Ransome who felt the loss of baby Donald (and though Mr Ransome would have been no joke as a father) a son might have knocked the corners off him a little and made life messier – tidiness and order now all that mattered to him in middle age. When you come down to it, what he is being condemned for here is not having got out of his shell, and had there been a child there might have been no shell.

Now he lies dumb and unmoving in Intensive Care and 'shell' seems to describe it pretty well. Somewhere he can hear his wife's voice, near but at the same time distant and echoing a little as if his ear was a shell too and he a creature in it. The nurses have told Mrs Ransome that he can certainly hear what she is saying, and thinking that he may not survive not so much the stroke as the shame and humiliation that attended it, Mrs Ransome concentrates on clearing that up first. 'If we can get on a more sensible footing in the sex department,' she thinks, 'we may end up regarding this stroke business as a blessing.'

So, feeling a little foolish that the conversation has of necessity to be wholly one-sided, Mrs Ransome begins to talk to her inert husband, or rather, since there are other patients in the ward, murmur in his ear; from the corner of his left eye Mr Ransome's view of her just the slightly furry powdered slope of her well-meaning cheek.

She tells him how she has known about what she calls 'his silliness' for years and that there is nothing to feel ashamed of, for it's only sex after all. Inside his shell Mr Ransome is trying to think what 'ashamed' is, and even 'feeling' he's no longer quite sure about, let alone 'sex'; words seem to have come unstuck from their meanings. Having been sensible about Mr Ransome's silliness just about brings Mrs Ransome to the end of her emotional vocabulary; never having talked about this kind of thing much leaves her for a moment at a loss for words. Still, Mr Ransome, though numb, is at the same time hurting and they plainly need to talk. So, holding his limp hand lightly in hers, Mrs Ransome begins to whisper to him in that language which she can see now she was meant to acquire for just this sort of eventuality.

'I find it hard to verbalise with you, Maurice,' she begins. 'We've always found it hard to verbalise with each other, you and me, but we are going to learn, I promise.' Pressing her lips up against his unflinching ear she sees in close-up the stiff little grey hairs he regularly crops with the curved scissors during his locked sessions in the bathroom. 'The nurses tell me you will learn to talk again, Maurice, and I will learn along with you, we will learn to talk to one another together.' The words swirl around his ear, draining into it uncomprehended. Mrs Ransome speaks slowly. It is like spooning pap into the mouth of a baby; as one wipes the mouth of the untaken food so Mrs Ransome could almost wipe the ear clean of the curd of the unheeded words.

Still, and she deserves credit for this, she persists.

'I'm not going to be, you know, judgmental, Maurice, because I personally have nothing to be judgmental about.' And she tells him how she too has secretly listened to the cassette.

'But in future, Maurice, I suggest we listen to it together, make it a part of honing up on our marital skills . . . because at the end of the day, love, marriage is about choices and to get something out of it you have to put something in.'

Out it tumbles, the once tongue-tied Mrs Ransome now possessed of a whole lexicon of caring and concern which she pours into her husband's ear. She talks about perspectives and sex and how it can go on joyful and unrestrained until the very brink of the grave and she adumbrates a future of which this will be a part and how once he gets back on his feet they will set aside quality time which they will devote to touching one another.

'We have never hugged, Maurice. We must hug one another in the future.'

Festooned as he is with tubes and drains and monitors, hugging Mr Ransome ill is no easier than hugging Mr Ransome well, so Mrs Ransome contents herself with kissing his hand. But having shared with him her vision of the future – tactile, communicative, convivial – she now thinks to top it off with some *Così*. It might just do the trick, she thinks.

So, careful not to dislodge any other of Mr Ransome's many wires, which are not channels of entertainment at all, Mrs Ransome gently positions the earphones on his head. Before slipping the cassette into the player she holds it before his unblinking eyes.

'Così,' she articulates. And more loudly: 'Mozart?'

She switches it on, scanning her husband's unchanging face for any sign of response. There is none. She turns the volume up a little, but not loud, mezzo forte, say. Mr Ransome, who has heard the word 'Mozart' without knowing whether it is a person or a thing or even an articulated lorry, now cringes motionless before a barrage of sounds that are to him utterly meaningless and that have no more pattern or sense than the leaves on a tree, only the leaves on the tree seem to be the notes and there is someone in the tree (it is Dame Kiri) shrieking. It is baffling. It is terrible. It is loud.

Perhaps it is this last awful realisation that Mozart does not make sense or it is because Mrs Ransome, finding there is still no response, decides to up the volume yet further, just as a last shot, that the sounds vibrate in Mr Ransome's ears and it is the vibration that does it; but at any rate something happens in his head, and the frail sac into which the blood has leaked now bursts, and Mr Ransome hears, louder and more compelling than any music he has ever heard, a roaring in his ears; there is a sudden brief andante, he coughs quietly and dies.

Mrs Ransome does not immediately notice that the numb hand of her husband is now not even that; and it would be hard to tell from looking at him, or from feeling him even, that anything has happened. The screen has altered but Mrs Ransome does not know about screens. However since Mozart does not seem to be doing the trick she takes the earphones from her husband's head and it's only as she is disentangling the frivolous wires from the more serious ones that she sees something on the screen is indeed different and she calls the nurse.

Marriage to Mrs Ransome had often seemed a kind of parenthesis and it's fitting that what she says to the nurse ('I think he's gone') is here in parenthesis too, and that it is this last little parenthesis that brings the larger parenthesis to a close.

The nurse checks the monitor, smiles sadly and puts a caring hand on Mrs Ransome's shoulder, then pulls the curtain round and leaves husband and wife alone together for the last time. And so, the brackets closed that opened 32 years before, Mrs Ransome goes home a widow.

Then there is a fitting pause. And television having schooled her in the processes of bereavement and the techniques of grieving, Mrs Ransome observes that pause; she gives herself ample time to mourn and to come to terms with her loss and generally speaking where widowhood is concerned she does not put a foot wrong.

It seems to her as she looks back that the burglary and everything that has happened since has been a kind of apprenticeship. Now, she thinks, I can start.

'The Clothes They Stood Up In' was first published in the London Review of Books on 28 November 1996.
The London Review of Books may be ordered through your local newsagent or taken on subscription. For subscriptions please call on 0171 209 1141 or Fax 0171 209 1151